Herobrine – Birth of a Monster

Barry J McDonald

DEDICATION

This book is dedicated to you, thank you!

Chapter 1

Herobrine looked at his huge home in the distance and smiled. It had taken a long time to build but now that it was finished it looked impressive. Anyone looking at this great structure would assume that it's owner must be a great Minecraft player. But like everyone else, Herobrine had lost count of how many times he'd died and respawned because of stupid mistakes. Whether that was by making poor shelter decisions, falling into a lava pit or not paying attention to his health bar. He had made all those noob mistakes. But that was in the past. Now that he had more experience under his belt he felt pretty confident about himself.

Last night had been a busy night. Creepers, zombies, and spiders had attacked him with the intention of wrecking his happy home. Playing the attack over in his mind Herobrine remarked at how well organized the group had been. Long gone were the days when they would come independent of each other shuffling toward him with no real goal? Now they seemed more precise in their movements, like someone or something was behind them pulling their strings and making decisions for them.

Herobrine yawned. He hadn't had much sleep this past few nights, but that was what happened when you played the game in survival mode. Thinking on this Herobrine wondered if there ever was a time when players didn't fear walking in the dark. "Probably be boring for you Wolfie," Herobrine said to his dog. "Come on let's go, that suns starting to go down."

Watching Wolfie run on ahead Herobrine remarked that taming a wolf was the best thing he'd done so far in the game. It could be lonely in Minecraft with players always coming and going. Some friends he knew gave up on the game because they found it too tough and never came back. Others never changed their spawn point and ended up back where they started never to be seen again. It was hard making and keeping friends in this world and this was what Herobrine loved about Wolfie. Apart from the company on those lonely nights in Minecraft he was much more than that. Wolfie had saved him many times in battle with hostile mobs and unfriendly locals. Herobrine remarked to himself how lucky he'd been to come upon the right wolf that day.

When they got back inside the safety of his home, Herobrine headed straight to Wolfie's favourite room, the kitchen. "You hungry boy?" Herobrine asked, scratching Wolfie behind the ear. "OK, let's see what we have tonight." Searching through his food stock Herobrine turned back to his dog with disappointment. "Sorry, boy its pork again. I was sure we had some fish or meat back there. Maybe tomorrow we can go out hunting and find something different to eat. What do you think?" Herobrine watched as Wolfie leapt for joy and barked back in response. "OK, OK, it's a date then."

Putting two large juicy pieces of pork on the furnace, Herobrine left them to sizzle and checked his armoury for weapons. If last night were anything to go by he knew they'd need their energy levels high. Looking in his armoury Herobrine found it was still well stocked with everything he could need. He hoped. You could never be sure nowadays. Even the best made plans still went wrong sometimes. Putting that thought to the back of his mind and happy that he was prepared as best a player could be. Herobrine went back to his other priority, feeding himself.

Clearing the table of what was left of his supper, Herobrine knew it was time to do his night time patrol. One thing he'd learned after all those respawnings was that it was always wise to check your perimeter wall and escape tunnels for damage and nasty surprises. From experience the last thing you needed was to get killed and lose everything because you were too stupid to check everything in advance.

After checking that all his escape routes were clear and free from danger, he started to relax. "Come on boy let's grab a few minutes of sleep before it all kicks off," Herobrine said and headed off in the direction of his bedroom. One good thing about having a dog was their keen sense of hearing and Herobrine knew that Wolfie would let him know the second he heard any danger.

Later that night Herobrine awoke from a deep sleep and found Wolfie growling. "Are they back again boy?" Herobrine asked looking in the direction Wolfie was growling. Rubbing the sleep from his eyes and stretching his muscles to wake them, Herobrine remarked that he didn't feel like he'd been asleep for long. Going to the window of his room he could see the pitch black of darkness outside. It must have been the early hours of the morning. "Showtime," Herobrine said to himself and ran to the door picking up his bow and arrows along the way. Running up the stairs to the highest battlements of his home. Herobrine stared out into the darkness beyond. "I wonder what they've planned for us tonight boy," Herobrine said to Wolfie. Wolfie growled deep in his throat as a response. "Well, let them come!" Herobrine said and loaded his bow with it first arrow.

Chapter 2

Herobrine listened to the night air and heard the usual moaning, hissing, and groaning sounds he'd come to know as trouble. In the early days those sounds used to send his pulse racing wildly and make his hands shake uncontrollably. Sometimes so badly that aiming a bow was an impossible task for him. But now things were a lot different. While those noises didn't scare him as much as they used to, he knew to still take things seriously. Just because he didn't fear hostile mobs anymore he still knew to pay them some respect. Showing off and being too cocky was always a recipe for disaster. In his eyes it was always better to either avoid trouble or at least keep it at a bow and arrow distance.

Herobrine turned to Wolfie when he heard him growl again. He knew his dog could sense the hostile mobs forming up outside the perimeter wall beyond the light of his torches. "We're safe boy don't worry. Let them make the first move and then we'll know what we're up against," Herobrine said. Thinking on what he'd just said to Wolfie, Herobrine remarked on how he'd wished someone else had told him this earlier in the game. There had been times in past when he'd allowed his imagination to get the better of him. Creating huge armies of hostile mobs in his mind when in fact there'd only been five or ten. From experience Herobrine knew it was best just to sit back and wait. Looking back out into the dark he wondered if they were trying to lure him out wanting him to make a mistake. Well they'd have to wait, because he wasn't as dumb as he used to be.

With no sign of danger coming to his front wall, Herobrine took a quick run around his battlements for any hostile mobs who may be coming from other directions. Living on his own had its advantages, but it also had its disadvantages. One of them was he couldn't look out in all directions at the same time. "Looks like they're only coming from the front tonight Wolfie. And it's a small-group too," Herobrine said with a grin. "They must have learned their lesson from last night." Taking no chances, Herobrine made sure he had his supply of bows, arrows, and swords spread around the perimeter wall for whenever they might be needed.

Then without warning the first arrow came through the darkness intent on hitting him. "Wow, that one was close!" Herobrine remarked as he watched it fly past him. "I guess we've some skeletons tonight." Taking his time Herobrine pulled his bow string back as far as it would go and launched his first arrow. Watching it disappear Herobrine heard a small groan in the dark which meant it had hit his target. "Guess he won't be firing any more arrows tonight," Herobrine said and laughed to himself. As Herobrine waited for battle to commence he was surprised when nothing else happened. For whatever reason the hostile mobs didn't seem interested in him anymore. Then to add to Herobrine's confusion Wolfie started to bark.

"Quiet boy, we don't want to draw attention to ourselves. What is it?" Looking in the same direction as Wolfie's ears were cocked, Herobrine strained to hear what his dog had heard. Hearing nothing at first Herobrine thought his dog was starting to lose its mind. Then as time passed he began to hear something on the night-time breeze. "Help, help me, oh somebody please help me!" Although faint at first there was no mistaking it. Someone was out there and they were in big trouble.

Chapter 3

How many times had he heard the words "Help me!" screamed out in Minecraft? In his earlier days he'd cried many times himself. Once it had been when he'd been found himself surrounded by creepers with no escape or weapon. Another time he'd found himself falling through space into a deep mineshaft. Minecraft could be a cruel world when it wanted to be. That was unless you knew the rules of survival and you stuck to them. But even then you still could get killed very easily.

"I know what you're thinking Wolfie, we should head out there and save them right. Do you want us to risk everything to save someone we don't know?" Herobrine had watched other players get killed before but he'd never taken any satisfaction in it. Sometimes he'd been too far away to help, other times he'd watched a new player not take good advice and die because of it. He knew it was all part of the game but that didn't make it any easier to watch.

Feeling his conscious get the better of him Herobrine groaned to himself. "Alright then but just this once. Let's go boy," Herobrine said and made his way towards one of his escape tunnels. Although he'd checked the tunnel earlier in the night. Herobrine still took out his sword before entering. Holding his torch high above his head Herobrine ran through the tunnel with Wolfie at his heels. When they'd reached the end Herobrine paused for a second before putting his foot on a pressure plate. "I hope this one's worth it boy. If we lose it all because of this stupid mistake I'll never forgive myself. Or you for that matter," Herobrine said to Wolfie, "Now don't look at me like that. This was your idea as much as it was mine!"

Taking his time Herobrine slowly raised his head up out of the tunnels trap door and into the night time air. Going from the brightness of the tunnel to the darkness above Herobrine had to wait until his eyes adjusted. It probably would have been wiser to use his torch for better light but that wasn't a risk he wanted to take. The last thing he needed was drawing attention to himself. Turning his head a full 360-degree turn Herobrine took in what was around him. Thankfully his home looked OK and the small group of hostile mobs hadn't noticed him. "OK I'm here now so where are you," Herobrine said to himself. Seeing and hearing nothing, Herobrine feared the worst and presumed that the player had met their death. Then almost as if they'd read his mind, the mysterious voice cried out again.

"Help me - -" Hearing the voice again Herobrine could sense the difference in its tone. To him it sounded like the player had given up all hope of ever finding help and was giving up. "OVER HERE, OVER HERE!" Herobrine shouted back. Hearing himself shout like that surprised Herobrine as he hadn't planned to drawing attention to himself. "OH PLEASE... WHERE ARE YOU…? I CAN'T SEE YOU… THEY'RE EVERYWHERE!" the voice screamed back. "So much for Plan A," Herobrine said pulling out his torch and waving it over his head. Now everyone hostile mob in the area would know where he was.

Out of the dark Herobrine could see the player turn and start to run in his direction. The bad news was, coming close behind he could see two skeletons in hot pursuit. This was going to be a close call. "RUN!" Herobrine screamed hoping in some way it might make the player run even faster. Before he knew it the player was on top of him diving head first through the open trap door. "THE PRESSURE PLATE. HIT THE PRESSURE!" Herobrine screamed and watched as the trap door closed tightly over his head.

"Whew, that was way too close for comfort," Herobrine said getting back on his feet. "Quickly let's get out of here. If any creepers get a scent of us they'll explode this tunnel down around our ears." Grabbing his new guest by the arm Herobrine guided her quickly back to his home. On reaching the end of the escape tunnel Herobrine let out a sigh of relief. "Please say that's the only excitement they've planned for us tonight. Wolfie you keep our guest company while I go to the wall and see what's happening outside," Herobrine said and ran off to check for trouble.

Looking down he could see the hostile mobs were in confusion. Although waving the torch and shouting out had seemed like a dangerous thing to do, it wasn't. Herobrine could now see that every hostile mob was now heading to the source of the noise and away from his home. Happy that things had worked out well Herobrine smiled to himself. Now that daylight was also breaking through things were starting to look up. "We live to fight another day," Herobrine said to himself and then headed back down to introduce himself to his new guest.

Chapter 4

"I don't know how to thank you… you saved my life," the girl said. Herobrine blushed. He didn't feel like a hero he was just doing the right thing. "I'm not one for heroics but I just couldn't let those things get their hands on you," Herobrine said. "So what's your name? I'm Herobrine and that cute mutt beside you is Wolfie." On hearing this Wolfie stared up at Herobrine as if he knew what he'd just said. "OK, OK, you're not a mutt. I was just kidding," Herobrine said and started to laugh. "Don't listen to him Wolfie I think you're cute. By the way my name's SparkleGirl23, but most people just call me SparkleGirl," the player said and held out her hand.

Getting the formality of shaking hands out of the way, Herobrine had a lot of questions he wanted answers to. "I take it you're only new to the game with a name like that," Herobrine asked. Herobrine could usually tell how long a player had been in Minecraft. The early players usually only had a name and that was it. But the later players who'd joined the Minecraft world usually had weirder names made up of combinations of numbers and letters. "This is my first week," SparkleGirl replied. "I'd tried building a shelter but as you can see it wasn't a very good one and I had to run for it. I was running around blindly until I saw your home in the distance. If you hadn't saved me, I don't know what I would have done."

Although Herobrine had promised that he'd never take another noob under his care, there was something about SparkleGirl he liked. "It's usually only me and Wolfie here, but if you want you can stay and you get your health level back up. And anyway the added company would probably do me and Wolfie some good," Herobrine said. "Oh thank you. I don't know what to say. But thank you," SparkleGirl said her face starting to blush. "Stop please, you're going to give me a big head. Come on let's go to the kitchen I've a couple of spare pork chops that I think we could all do with right now."

As Herobrine made breakfast for everyone SparkleGirl told him all about herself. She told him of that first scary night when she'd struggled to build a shelter and the silly mistakes she'd made before he'd saved her. "Don't be embarrassed we all make stupid mistakes in the early days. I would be embarrassed to tell you about all the crazy things I did. But over time you'll learn from your mistakes and they don't happen as often. If you want, I'll be happy to show you a thing or two while you stay here," Herobrine added. "That would be great Herobrine. I guess this is my lucky day meeting someone like you. You could've watched and let those skeletons use me for target practice but you didn't. That says a lot about you," SparkleGirl said. Herobrine blushed, he wasn't used to getting so many compliments in one day. "Come on, eat up and we'll start your training after breakfast," Herobrine said clearing away the breakfast dishes.

*****

Herobrine and SparkleGirl spent the rest of the day going over the basics of survival in Minecraft. "Wow, you pick up things really quickly SparkleGirl. That would have taken me longer to learn all that when I was a beginner," Herobrine said impressed with his new student. "Naw, you must be just a great teacher Herobrine. I think that's what it is. Now come on teach me something more," SparkleGirl said. "I'd love to, but as you can see the suns starting to go down. It's time to get ready for the night ahead. Ever fired a bow before?" Herobrine asked. "No," SparkleGirl said. "But I'm sure you could teach me in no time." "Well if tonight's anything like the last few nights you'll have plenty of targets to shoot at," Herobrine added, "Come on let's get a meal inside you and then we'll go over our plan for tonight."

After supper Herobrine showed SparkleGirl his night time routine. First stop was to check all escape routes were clear of danger. Then it was off to the armoury for a quick weapon check. Then finally he made sure he had weapons close at hand at all times. "You can't prepare for everything that might happen SparkleGirl. But doing this makes sure we've got most things covered. After that sometimes it's just down to luck. Now it's time to make you a bed and we can all get some sleep. Well for a little while anyway," Herobrine said with a smile.

Lying in bed later that night Herobrine suddenly had a bad feeling come over him. In the back of his mind like an itch he couldn't scratch, a small part of him felt that something bad was about to happen. At first he pushed the thought away but he knew to trust his instincts. They had saved him many times before in the past. Probably just tiredness, Herobrine thought to himself before falling asleep.

Chapter 5

Like the night before, Wolfie's bark warned Herobrine of oncoming danger. Running across the courtyard Herobrine met SparkleGirl already awake and rubbing her eyes. "The barking what's happening," she asked. "Hostile mobs are on the way SparkleGirl. You'd better get prepared for what's ahead," Herobrine said and gave her a sword and a bow.

Standing on the high perimeter wall Herobrine, SparkleGirl, and Wolfie looked out in the distance. The darkness didn't give much away but they could all sense the hostile mobs getting ready for an attack. "I'm sorry I didn't have enough time to teach you more. Just do the best you can SparkleGirl. But if anything happens to me just make for one of the escape tunnels and take Wolfie with you. He knows the way out and he'll protect you," Herobrine remarked patting his dog on the side. "Don't talk like that Herobrine we'll be fine here. Just look at those walls nothing can get into this place," SparkleGirl said pointing to the walls that surrounded her. "Don't ever take your safety for granted SparkleGirl. I've seen bigger places than this fall to hostile mobs. Now stay here while I check the other walls for activity," Herobrine said and ran along the battlements.

Looking around his home Herobrine got an uneasy feeling that his home was being surrounded. Returning to SparkleGirl he gave her the bad news. "It doesn't look too bad out there but I don't know for sure. They could be getting organized in the dark and we wouldn't know," Herobrine said. As he said those words the darkness around his home seemed to move toward them.

Then without warning three arrows came flying from the darkness and headed their way. "GET DOWN!" Herobrine screamed just in time to see one arrow fly over SparkleGirl's head. "I think it's best if you keep your head down and just supply me with arrows while I get busy with my bow," Herobrine said loading his first arrow into his bow. Holding his bow in his hands Herobrine remarked to himself on how he loved using it. Over the many weeks he'd lived in Minecraft he'd become a crack shot with it. In some ways he preferred it to his sword. While using a sword took skill he found that taking down a hostile mob from a long distance away was even more satisfying.

Looking over his wall Herobrine could see that this was no disorganized mob below him. Like before they looked too well organized. There has to be someone out there putting this rag-tag group into order, Herobrine wondered, but why. Why someone would be out there testing him night after night it just didn't make sense. Putting all those questions to the back of his mind Herobrine grabbed his bow tightly and got ready for his first target.

He didn't have to wait long before a skeleton came racing out of the dark intent on doing harm. Without wasting a second Herobrine quickly took aim and launched his arrow. It was a good shot that sent the skeleton flying backwards on its back dead. After that it all quickly became a blur. Wave after wave of creepers, zombies, and skeletons came charging from all directions. Because Herobrine knew he was well outnumbered he picked his fight well. While the skeletons caused plenty of trouble with all their flying arrows it was the creepers that Herobrine was more worried about. One hole blown in his wall or a door taken down and his home could easily be overrun. "We're going to need every arrow we have SparkleGirl. It's going to be a long night tonight," Herobrine said and watched as SparkleGirl ran off to bring back as many arrows as she could carry.

When she returned SparkleGirl found Herobrine down to his last arrow and sweat pouring from his brow. "This is harder than I thought it was going to be. Whoever is behind all of this is really trying to tire me out," Herobrine said. "They don't seem to care about these mobs. They just keep on coming." A battle even a battle in Minecraft had some satisfaction if it was for a good cause Herobrine thought. But this fight wasn't. Although the bodies of the hostile mobs had faded away to nothing Herobrine could still feel their death lingering on in the surrounding air. Then just when things seemed like they were going his way his luck changed.

Chapter 6

Whether it was bad luck or taking the health of his weapon for granted, but Herobrine now found himself with a broken bow. "Damn!" Herobrine swore to himself as he watched the creeper he would have shot now standing right at his wall. With barely a moment to spare Herobrine screamed a warning just before the creeper exploded punching a hole in his perimeter wall.

Without wasting a moment Herobrine raced down the stairway as fast as he could to the source of the damage. He may have had escape tunnels to escape to, but they weren't in his mind right now. This was his home and he was going to protect it with his life if he had to. Arriving at the place where the wall had been breached, Herobrine could see all the hostile mobs outside start to change direction and move toward the wounded wall. "What will we do Herobrine? Is it time to go to the escape tunnel?" SparkleGirl called to him above all the noise. "You go and take Wolfie with you. Head to the tunnel and run quickly!" he screamed back. Without waiting for an answer Herobrine ran to find a nearby sword and got ready for action. "If they want a fight, then that's what I'll give them," Herobrine said running to face the hostile mobs.

Through both anger and a kind of energy he didn't know he had, Herobrine slashed his way through the hostile mobs. A skeleton who had assumed the coast was clear paid for its mistake by losing his head. After that a nearby zombie was stopped in his tracks with a quick stab to its belly. Before he knew it Herobrine found himself facing waves of creepers, zombies, and skeletons without no sign of it ending.

While Herobrine had been a fit match until now, he began feeling his energy level drop and his sword arm begin to slow. Maybe he should have gone into the escape tunnel with SparkleGirl and Wolfie. It was just a house and he could build another one. But by now it was too late and he was too deep in the fight to give up now.

Like the sea going in and out, some battles seem to go one way and then suddenly change back. Where once the hostile mobs seemed to have the upper hand, it then changed back in Herobrine's favour. But now it looked like the hostile mobs were in command of things again. Herobrine could feel it in the way they grew in confidence. Some mobs going to the left to distract him while others went to the right to get past him. Fighting as close as he could to the gap in the wall, Herobrine tried his best to block the way inside. The only problem was he was only one person with one set of eyes. Herobrine watched as if in slow motion as his battle with a skeleton when interrupted by a pair of red eyes that came into view.

A spider, so this is how it was going to end, Herobrine thought to himself as he cut through the skeleton. Knowing he wouldn't have enough time to prepare for the fight with the spider Herobrine closed his eyes and waited for death. He'd fought well but sometimes that wasn't good enough. Counting the seconds over in his head Herobrine waited until he'd be respawning back in his bed. Then surprisingly nothing happened. Opening one eye Herobrine stood and wondered what had happened. He'd been expecting his death to come quickly, but all he saw was a dead spider fading away in front of him. Had the spider been shot by a stray arrow from its own kind, he wondered.

"RUN YOU FOOL, DON'T JUST STAND THERE!" Herobrine turned to see SparkleGirl standing behind him lowering her bow. "Come on. Are you going to help me or what?" she said loading her bow. For a split second Herobrine stood frozen in confusion. "Er yeah, coming," was all he could think of saying before he ran to take his place beside her. "You didn't think I'd really leave, did you," SparkleGirl said firing another arrow into the head of an oncoming creeper. "Where did you learn to shoot like that?" Herobrine asked. "No time for small talk. There's a battle going on here and we're going to win it," SparkleGirl said with a huge grin on her face.

Whether it had been the death of the spider or the loss of so many, but Herobrine could see the battle had now been won. "We did it. We did it!" SparkleGirl cried jumping up and down in excitement. Herobrine let out a sigh of relief as he watched the last of the hostile mobs begin to leave. He hadn't felt this tired in a long while and bet his health level had almost bottomed out. Although he was too tired to think and drained from battle, there was something that stuck in his mind.

Where did SparkleGirl learn to shoot a bow like that? He hadn't taught her and that wasn't beginners luck she'd had. Was there something else going on that he didn't know about? Herobrine decided that he was too tired to think about it now. First he'd get the wall fixed and then get some sleep. Thinking and talking could come later.

Chapter 7

By the time Herobrine woke from his sleep the sun was already starting to go down. "What, how, aargh!" Herobrine exclaimed and jumped out of bed. Running outside he found SparkleGirl and Wolfie sitting enjoying supper in the last rays of the setting sun. "What, you never woke me SparkleGirl. We need to prepare for tonight. What if it's going to be as bad as last night? We've wasted all those hours!" Herobrine said annoyed with the two of them. "Don't worry Herobrine, Wolfie and I've been busy. Your supper is waiting on the furnace and I've already checked all escape tunnels and weapon levels. We may be a bit low on arrows but that's all you will need to take care of. Now go get your supper," SparkleGirl said with a smile. "Go on, off you go." On hearing this Herobrine began to relax a little. "Thanks… I." "Go get your supper we've everything in hand here," SparkleGirl said scratching Wolfie under the chin. Still in shock at how well she'd handed things, Herobrine left to find his supper and then came back out to join them with his meal.

"Do you think they'll be back again?" SparkleGirl asked. "I don't know it's hard to tell. I used to look forward to those nights when I had something to fight. But now I'd just like a few boring nights where nothing happens," Herobrine said eating his supper as fast he could. Waiting while he got his meal out of the way Herobrine knew he'd have to ask the question.

"So how did you ever learn to fire a bow like that? That was a difficult shot you took and you could have hit me in the process but you didn't. So am I missing something here or have you been telling me the truth SparkleGirl?" Herobrine asked. For a second SparkleGirl looked away and then turned back to face him. "I guess it was just beginners luck. I was watching you use your bow so much, I must have picked up some tips along the way," Sparkle said with a little redness showing in her cheeks. Although Herobrine didn't want to come straight out and call SparkleGirl a liar, it just didn't seem like she was telling the truth.

"Are you lying to me SparkleGirl?" Herobrine asked. SparkleGirl blushed even more when she heard this and took a moment to answer him. "Really, it was beginners luck Herobrine. You told me you had your eyes closed at the time, so how do you know it was such a difficult shot," SparkleGirl replied. Herobrine had to admit his eyes had been closed so maybe she was right maybe the shot hadn't been a difficult one. Maybe the spider had given SparkleGirl a bigger target to hit than he'd thought. "I'm sorry I just thought well, I don't know what I really thought... sorry," Herobrine said now getting embarrassed that he'd asked. "That's fine let's not worry about that right now. Come on we need to get ready for tonight," SparkleGirl said getting up and dusting herself down.

With most of the things already organized and put away. Herobrine concentrated on the low supply of arrows they'd in stock. "Do you think we have enough this time Herobrine?" SparkleGirl asked looking over the pile of arrows he'd created. "Who knows? If it's going to be like last night probably not. But if things get really bad its best if we use the escape tunnel this time. My stubbornness last night almost got me killed, and that's one mistake I'm not going to make tonight. Come on let's get some sleep. We could do with it," Herobrine replied.

*****

Herobrine woke in the middle of the night and looked around him. That's strange he thought to himself, Wolfie would usually be up and barking by now. Although he trusted Wolfie with his life Herobrine still got out of bed and headed to the high wall to check for danger. It was a quiet night which was weird for Minecraft. There always seemed to be at least a handful of hostile mobs wandering around looking for trouble. But tonight nothing. While a quiet night was welcomed by Herobrine it still didn't give him any peace of mind. If someone were out there controlling hostile mobs it also seemed like they could hold them back when they wanted to. And if they were holding them back, what was the reason.

Whatever the reason, this peaceful night was welcomed. Herobrine's food stocks had been getting very low and he needed to go out hunting. All the fighting and repair work had been a distraction that had taken him away from his survival needs. "Can't sleep?" Herobrine turned with a start, sword at the ready. "I never heard you coming up behind me. You're as quiet as a cat SparkleGirl you know that. So you couldn't sleep either?" "It would be hard to relax after the night we had. I lay there tossing and turning wondering what else was coming our way," SparkleGirl added. "I need to go out tomorrow SparkleGirl. I've been neglecting our food stocks for a while now and I need to get around to it. Will you be all right here on your own? I could leave Wolfie here with you if you want the company?" Herobrine asked. "Don't worry I'll be fine. You know what, take Wolfie with you if you want. You told me he's a good hunting dog so bring him. I bet he'll enjoy it," SparkleGirl said. "And anyway I'm a big girl so what could go wrong." "Well if you're sure that's OK," Herobrine asked surprised by her reply, "It looks like it's going to be a quiet night tonight so I'll leave at daybreak. Try to get a little sleep and I'll see you in the morning." "Maybe tonight's the night that everything starts to get better," SparkleGirl called after him.

Maybe, but I doubt it, Herobrine thought, that would be too easy.

Chapter 8

It was nice to wake in the morning feeling fresh and well rested, and that's how Herobrine felt right now. He missed waking up like this, but that was the nature of the game. Survival was the mode his was in and that was the one he liked. Peaceful mode was fun, but it never tested you or made you a stronger player. If you could take everything that Minecraft could give you in survival mode and still come out on top. You were a true Minecraft player in Herobrine's eyes.

"Ready to stretch those legs of yours Wolfie?" Herobrine asked sitting on the edge of his bed. On hearing this Wolfie leapt around in excitement barking for all he was worth. He loved running free in the world beyond the walls following scents and hunting game, that was when he was at his happiest. Grabbing his bow and packing a small amount of food rations and water, Herobrine went to find SparkleGirl. "Morning sleepy head. Come on get up the day's almost over," he joked pulling the blanket off her. "Are you sure you'll be OK? I mean if you've changed your mind about me heading out, please tell me." "Don't worry about me Herobrine. I'll be fine," she said. "I promise I won't set foot outside the wall. Now go have fun," SparkleGirl giggled seeing Wolfie's excitement. "Alright then. See you later!" Herobrine said heading off in the direction of the main gate.

Opening the gate Herobrine took a deep breath of fresh air. He missed the world outside and the freedom to go in any direction he wanted. Home was fine, but he loved to explore. This was where he was able to relax and it also gave him time to think. This was what he needed right now time to think. Although Herobrine had taken SparkleGirl at her word something still didn't feel right about her. She'd told him she'd been a new player, but the way she handled a bow. Then there was the way she quickly mastered crafting. She was either a very good student or knew more than she was letting on. Then again maybe he was looking for something that wasn't there.

Letting these thoughts go from his mind Herobrine got back to the matter in hand looking for food. It didn't take long before Wolfie caught a scent of something and he let out a bark. "Go on do your magic. Off you --!"

Herobrine was about to say before Wolfie took off without waiting for an answer. Over the time they'd worked together Herobrine and Wolfie had worked out a system. It wasn't much of a system but it worked well. Wolfie working like a sheep dog would herd the pigs or cattle into a small group and send them back in Herobrine's direction. There Herobrine would be waiting with a freshly dug pit to trap them in. Then it was just a simple job of shooting all the animals that had fallen in. It was a simple idea that worked well. And Herobrine liked simple ideas.

Standing by his freshly dug pit Herobrine waited impatiently for Wolfie's return. There was no sign of him. "Where did you get to," Herobrine swore, "After all this digging and you go walkabout. You and I are going to have some words mister." Fed up and giving up on the idea that Wolfie was coming back to him. Herobrine ran off in the last direction he'd seen him go. Climbing to the top of the closest hill, Herobrine stopped to catch his breath and scanned the countryside below. "What the…" Herobrine exclaimed seeing a farm house that lay in ruin.

Curious to see what had happened to it, he made his way downhill. Now closer Herobrine could see the tell-tale signs of an attack. It didn't look good. Whoever had done it had come at the house in great numbers and attacked it from all sides. Herobrine was doubtful anyone made it out alive. Looking around for any sign of activity, Herobrine spotted Wolfie also looking at the ruin. "Come here boy," Herobrine called to his dog. "Things don't look too good do they? I wonder if anyone's still alive. Let's go and check." As walk closer Herobrine could sense Wolfie thought that this was a bad idea. As the closer they got to the ruin the more his dog slowing its walk.

Now almost at the farmhouse, Herobrine could see that the destruction was even worse than he'd first thought. One end wall hung at a dangerous angle and going inside, Herobrine could see blue sky through a burnt out gap in the roof. Griefers! Herobrine thought. Herobrine hated griefers with a passion and often wondered why anyone would want to be one. What skill did you need taking things from others. The big guy taking from the little guy. It wasn't griefing it was just plain bullying. He'd been on the receiving side of them in the past and lost badly to them. To Herobrine they were worse scum than hostile mobs.

Although it was empty of people now Herobrine still felt like he shouldn't be there. Looking around him Herobrine could now see he'd been wrong with his first assumption. This wasn't a griefer attack it had been hostile mobs that had taken this place apart. Herobrine could see evidence of this. Unlike a griefer attack all the food stocks and weapons had been left untouched. But why, why attack this place with such vengeance, he wondered. Unless this had been a training exercise and someone was testing their tactics on helpless players. That was it.

He had been right. This was a sign that someone had an army and wasn't afraid to use it. This was no random group of hostile mobs wandering about. This group were organized and build for destruction. Standing in the ruin Herobrine suddenly got a sense that he was being watched. Wolfie had been right about this place there was danger still here. "Come on Wolfie let's grab as much food and weapons as we can take. We're going home right now," Herobrine said opening his inventory and loading it as quickly as he could.

Worried about SparkleGirl left all on her own Herobrine suddenly wanted to get back home as quickly as he could. Running from the farm house, Herobrine and Wolfie never slowed until they'd put a good distance between themselves and the ruin. Now far enough away Herobrine slowed down to a walking pace and tried to gather his thoughts. Who could behind all of this, he wondered, was his home next. He guessed he might never know the answers to those questions, but for now he had enough food to last him a while. Once he got back home everything would be better. He was sure of it.

Holding his hand over his eyes to protect them from the glare of the setting sun, Herobrine looked at his home in the distance. As he looked, he wondered what SparkleGirl might be getting up to. Was she practising her crafting skills, checking weapon levels or just putting up her feet? This made him smile. But that smile was soon wiped from his face when he noticed two players coming out of his main gate. He must be mistaken, he thought. Surely SparkleGirl wouldn't open the door to just anyone, would she. Herobrine squinted his eyes trying to overcome the brightness the brightness of the sun. His mind was playing tricks on him, that's what it was. Deciding not to take any chances Herobrine set off running as fast as he could in the direction of his home.

Chapter 9

By the time Herobrine reached his home he was out of breath. He had pushed himself hard in the run and could feel his energy level getting low. Looking around he could see no sign of any activity around his house. In fact, it looked just as when he'd left it. Putting his foot on the hidden pressure plate near the front gate, Herobrine called to Wolfie. "Come on boy, let's go and find SparkleGirl. I wonder what she's been up to while we've been away."

Standing inside his homes courtyard Herobrine wondered what he'd say to SparkleGirl. Should he come straight out and ask who the strangers coming out of his home were, or just play it cool and see if she told him. "SparkleGirl, where are you? We're back. Did you miss us," Herobrine called out. Nothing. This didn't make Herobrine feel any better about the situation. Where could she be, he wondered to himself. "Go find SparkleGirl boy. She must be hiding. Go find her," Herobrine said and watched as Wolfie picked up her scent and then raced off to find her.

As Wolfie left, Herobrine had a sense of dread come over him. Was there someone else here he didn't know about. Suddenly Herobrine was worried that he'd just sent Wolfie into a trap. He had grown to love the dog considerably and if anything happened to him, life in Minecraft wouldn't be the same anymore. Then to his relief he heard Wolfie barking loudly. The kitchen, that's where they were. Running off in that direction Herobrine wondered why SparkleGirl hadn't answered him. It's not like she couldn't hear him if she was close by, he wondered, so what was the reason.

On entering the kitchen Herobrine found SparkleGirl lying on the kitchen floor unconscious. "No!" Herobrine roared throwing himself on the ground beside her. Kneeling over her body he checked her over. She didn't seem to have any type of injury or wounds, so what had happened. Herobrine lowered his ear to SparkleGirl's mouth and found she was still breathing. She was still alive, but just about. Her breathing was very shallow and slow. Herobrine started to panic. Although he'd only known SparkleGirl a very short time he couldn't bear to see her like this. Lost in worry Herobrine wondered what to do next when Wolfie startled him with a growl. "What is it boy?" Herobrine asked running over to see what his dog was sniffing.

"Zombie flesh! How on earth did that find its way here," Herobrine said and his brain went into overdrive trying to put all the pieces of the puzzle together. There seemed to be only one conclusion, the strangers had left it. But right now that didn't matter. How the zombie flesh had made its way to the kitchen; he didn't know or care right now. SparkleGirl had eaten some of the flesh and was poisoned. How could she not have known to eat zombie flesh? It was such noob mistake, Herobrine wondered.

At that thought Herobrine felt a wave of guilt come over him. All this time he'd questioned SparkleGirl's experience in the game. How could he have thought she'd been lying to him when she'd made a mistake such as this? Looking at her lifeless body Herobrine wondered if she'd make it through the night. It was hard to say right now. Wondering he'd do next Herobrine went back and sat by her body. He could just sit here and watch her slowly slip away and respawn back in her bed. But why do that. It would be easy to sit back and do nothing but that wasn't the way Herobrine played the game.

Thinking for a while Herobrine wondered what he could do. Was there a cure for zombie flesh? The Nether that was it! He'd heard of a rare flower that had great healing properties in the Nether. It may have been just a rumour but it was worth checking out. Anything was better than just sitting around doing nothing. Lifting SparkleGirl's body off the floor Herobrine took her to her bed and made her comfortable. He knew she'd respawn back there if the worst happened, but somehow it felt better putting her there rather than leaving her lying on the floor.

Getting together everything he'd need, Herobrine quickly grabbed some food rations to boost his energy levels. Seeing all the sudden activity Wolfie started to wag his tail. "I'm sorry boy but you need to stay here. I'm going to have enough problems looking over my shoulder without worrying about you too. Anyway, SparkleGirl needs you. If she respawn's it would be nice to have a friendly face around when she wakes up." Wolfie whined a little when he heard this which made Herobrine smile. It seemed that Wolfie was trying to argue with him. "No boy, no arguments. This is a one-man job. Your job is to stay here."

Gathering his things and packed away his sword and bow Herobrine was ready. Going to the Nether didn't worry him that much. Yes it could be a scary place, but if you watched your back you could get safely through it and back. The only thing that worried him was looking for the flower. Did it exist, or was he just risking his life for nothing. This was the second time he was putting his neck on the line for SparkleGirl. But this time it was different he knew her now and she was worth it. Even with this strong reason Herobrine knew if he thought about it too long he'd probably talk himself out of his journey.

Opening his front gate again Herobrine looked at the darkening sky. It was getting dark and there'd probably be trouble out there waiting for him. But that wasn't going to stop him. Looking back one more time and thinking of the scene inside his home Herobrine took off in a quick sprint.

Chapter 10

Herobrine liked the area where he lived and compared to other places in Minecraft it felt like home. This had been one of the reasons he had built such a large home there. Another was its location close to mountains and caves that were brim full of iron ore and coal. It was in one of those caves where he had created his portal to the Nether.

Herobrine stood at the mouth of the cave and looked inside; all looked well. After getting all the way from his home without meeting any hostile mobs. Herobrine was expecting for the cave to make up for that. It had been a while since he'd been back to his cave and he wondered if it was as he left it. Who knew if any other Minecraft players had found the cave and plundered it of his stash of supplies? This was one of the reasons that he'd never placed torches near the entrance and only at the back. For fear that any passer-by would notice the light and be attracted to it. The only problem was, any hostile mob was also free to spawn there.

Making his way to the back of the cave Herobrine used his torch to find the way to the stairway that lead to his portal. Pausing for a second Herobrine sensed that something was wrong. The last time he'd been this deep in the cave he'd made sure that there was an adequate supply of torches lighting the way. But now nothing. Something wasn't right. Reaching down for the handle of his sword Herobrine took it out and held it in front of him. Just in case. Must be my crazy imagination, he thought to himself. With all that had happened lately it was understandable.

"Hello Herobrine. So good to meet you at last," a voice hissed from the darkness behind him. Spinning around Herobrine found himself face to face with a witch. "I didn't mean to scare you like that, but you'd probably get a scare no matter what I said," she remarked with a cackle. Before she could say another word Herobrine instantly got into his battle stance and swung his sword straight for the witch's neck. But it failed. With a loud thud Herobrine's sword harmlessly bounced off an invisible shield and rebounded backwards.

"Now that's not a nice way to say hello Herobrine. Especially as someone who has been taking such good care of you," the witch said pretending that her feelings were hurt. "You looked so lonely out there in that little home of yours. So I've been sending mobs to keep you company this past couple of nights."

Now everything clicked into place in Herobrine's mind. So this was the puppet master behind all those attacks on his home. A witch but why he wondered. Although Herobrine was curious as to the answer to that question. His instinct to kill the witch was even stronger. Holding his sword's hilt even tighter than the first time, he drew his sword back and swung with all his might in the direction of the witch. Nothing. Like the first time, his sword was easily deflected away. "Do you want to keep this up all night Herobrine? Believe me, you'll tire before you break this protective shield of mine. So do you want to keep going at this silly game or do you want answers to all your questions?" the witch asked. Herobrine thought over what the witch said; it looked like he was never going to hurt her, so maybe it was best to get answers first. Then when her defences were down, he'd attack!

"How do you know me? You know my name, you know where I live, but I know nothing about you," Herobrine said. "Oh I've been watching you a long time Herobrine. Like you I've been in the Minecraft world a long time. Back in the days when there were very few players coming in from the outside world. But now it's so much different. More and more of them are coming here taking our land, our food and plundering our caves of treasures. Thieves they are all of them. How dare they. And then they have the cheek to call us the Hostile ones!" the witch said and spat. "What's all of this got to do with me witch?" Herobrine asked. "You're different Herobrine. Unlike the others you kept to yourself. Yes you took land and you took food, but you didn't set out to find trouble and harm others without cause. While other players killed everything in sight. Even their own, to live here. You had a code that you kept to and I admire you for that," the witch said with a hint of a smile.

"So why have you been trying to kill me if you admire me so much?" Herobrine asked. "I'm afraid that wasn't my decision. There are others in our group who didn't support my thinking and wanted to test you. Was this great Herobrine the great warrior I had said you were? So I tested you. I sent hostile mobs at you to see how you could cope and you proved me right. You are indeed one of the better players in Minecraft, but you have one weakness, your heart. Your greatest gift is also your greatest weakness Herobrine," the witch added.

"At least I have a heart you old crone!" Herobrine snapped back, "You're no better than the players you speak of. They kill and plunder and you do the same." "I'm glad we've met tonight Herobrine. Because you're about to see how the outside world is about to rear its ugly head again. Taking and plundering without any cause or reason. You're about to see how foolish and weak you are Herobrine. Come with me," the witch said beckoning him to follow her. Although Herobrine didn't like taking commands from a witch he bit his tongue and followed her to the mouth of the cave. Then he would wait until the right moment and strike her down when she was least expecting it.

Herobrine stood by the witch and watched as she muttered to herself and made a floating cube of light appear out of nowhere and float in front of them. "Look into the cube Herobrine and you'll see what I say is true," the witch said with a sly grin. Staring intently Herobrine could make out a clear image of his home in the floating cube. "Yes that's my home. So what. What has this got to do with my great weakness," he asked and started to chuckle. "You've a lot to learn Herobrine. I think this is one lesson you'll remember for a long time," the witch snapped back. "Now look if you don't believe me!" Again Herobrine looked into the cube and found his home was still there. But things now looked a lot different. "Nooooo!" Herobrine cried out. This was his worst nightmare come true.

Little did he know his nightmare was about to get much worse.

Chapter 11

His beautiful home the one he had worked on for so long was now being looted and trashed. Herobrine stared in disbelief as he watched griefers entering and leaving with all that he owned. All that HE owned! The thought of this filled Herobrines body with so much hot rage he felt like he was full of lava from the Nether. "How dare they do this to me? They'll pay for this," he cursed at the image. Then just as quickly as his anger came, it left and he was filled with fear. Oh no, what about SparkleGirl and Wolfie what was happening to them. Were they putting up a fight, were they hurt? Images and thoughts flew through Herobrines mind quicker than he could keep up and he felt sick.

"SparkleGirl, Wolfie I must save them. They need me!" Herobrine cried to the witch. "You and I know you'll never be able to stop them Herobrine. By the time you get there it'll all be over. Think about it. You're vastly outnumbered. You'd never be able to fight them all. No you'll stay here with me and watch it unfold," she sneered. "I think you're in for a bit of a surprise Herobrine. Maybe you better keep watching."

Herobrine tried closing his eyes to keep out the scene of what was happening but couldn't. Parts of his home were now on fire and it looked like by morning it would all be gone. What once had been his stronghold would then be just a ruin. "Look closely Herobrine. I think you'll want to see what happens next," the witch said almost licking her lips. Suddenly Herobrine could see SparkleGirl and Wolfie coming out the gate. Oh thank God they're safe! he thought to himself. Looking in the cube he could see SparkleGirl holding Wolfie in her arms. Was he injured, he wondered. Then he watched in tears as he saw her run with Wolfie in her arms before stumbling and falling over.

"No!" Herobrine cried when he saw three players coming up behind her. With whatever magic the witch had used Herobrine could hear and see what was about to happen. "No please ChuckBone. I did what you said. You told me to come here and make friends with him and I did. But we were wrong he really is a good guy not an enemy. We didn't have to do this to him. We all could have worked together," SparkleGirl pleaded. "It looks like you've gone soft SparkleGirl. Did you forget all about us when you were living like a princess in your new castle?" At this all three players laughed. "Just leave me here and I won't say anything. Just leave before he gets back," she said. "He really fell for that zombie flesh trick didn't he? You're quite the actress SparkleGirl. Well there's been a change of plan and it doesn't include you or that mutt there," ChuckBone said pointing at SparkleGirl and Wolfie.

Herobrine knew what was about to happen next but prayed with all his might that he was wrong. Looking through eyes filled with hate, anger and betrayal he watched as Chuckbone pulled out his bow and shot SparkleGirl and Wolfie dead. "NOOOOOOOO!" Herobrine screamed and then dropped to his knees. Inside he felt like someone had just taken a large pin to him and he was deflating like a balloon.

Looking up and back into the cube Herobrine watched the three players walking away from SparkleGirl and Wolfie's bodies and heard one say "I wonder where SparkleGirl will respawn. Now that we've broken her bed here and the one back at the village. She'll probably never find her way back here again." "Ah who cares," another one said "She served her purpose and we got what we wanted."

"So much for your little friend Herobrine," the witch said. "See how she used you. She took you for a fool and she was so right. You've been too soft and now look at where it's left you. One of the greatest players in all of Minecraft now on his knees. It's not fair is it, but it doesn't always have to be like this. I know the great Minecraft player you can be with a little of my help. I can give you armies; I can give you power you only dreamed about. Never again will you ever have to fear or lose to your enemies. They'll run in front of you and you'll crush them like ants!"

"How, what will I have to give up for this power?" Herobrine asked his voice filled with rage. "Nothing Herobrine. All I asked is that you serve me. You'll be free to come and go through Minecraft as you please. But if and when I need you, you'll come to me. That's all I ask," the witch said. "Now come we must be quick. Let us not look on these painful scenes any longer. We've got plans to make. Revenge will be so so sweet!" the witch added with a large smile on her face.

Chapter 12

Herobrine felt numb now. As if someone had taken all his insides out and stuffed him full of cotton wool. There was so much going on that it felt like his mind was going to break under the strain. What had started off as a pretty normal day was now far from normal. His home was gone; his friend was gone and his dog was gone. There had been times in the past when his stupidity had caused him to lose everything. But this time it was different. This time it was far more painful and he'd lost so much more. In fact he felt like he'd lost part of himself in the attack.

"Come Herobrine. Follow me quickly!" the witch commanded "We must make for the Nether right now." Herobrine followed along shuffling behind the witch. He didn't care anymore if he was about to be killed, so be it. He wouldn't even put up a fight. "Come this way Herobrine and I'll show you how you'll have your revenge," the witch said taking Herobrine by the shoulder and pushing him gently into the shimmering pool of the portal.

After a second or two of being disorientated Herobrine blinked his eyes. Standing on the Nether side of the portal everything looked and felt exactly the same as the last time he'd been here. He could hear the sounds of lava bubbling nearby and feel the heat being given off by the rocks that surrounded him. But it wasn't. Compared to his earlier visits there were no hostile mobs anywhere. It was as if they all knew there was something evil in their presence and so kept away. Whoever this witch was she must have had great power. So why was he following her. Revenge that's what it was. He was looking for revenge for all the wrong that had been done to him," Herobrine thought numbly to himself.

After a short walk Herobrine and the witch came to a huge waterfall of lava. Looking up Herobrine marvelled at the beauty of it but also the danger it held. "This way Herobrine. My home is on the other side of that waterfall. Don't fear we'll not burn," she said and waved her hand to the side. Instantly the waterfall parted in the middle to reveal a tunnel entrance beyond it. "Come. Let me show you around my home and we'll make our plans."

31

The witch guided Herobrine to a large table that lay in the centre of a huge room. He'd been expecting the witch's home to be a place of squalor and decay, but was surprised to see how the walls of the cave had been beautifully carved with diamonds inset in them. Sitting back and taking in his surroundings he watched as the witch returned with a goblet that contained some type of gold liquid inside. "You speak of me having revenge witch. How. What do I need to do?" Herobrine asked confused. Some of his feeling of numbness had passed and now felt that he needed answers. "I told you Herobrine I can give you an army. An army that will run by your side. You'll have revenge for your friends like I promised. Then you are free to live where ever you want, knowing that nothing like this will ever happen to you again," she said putting the goblet down in front of him. "What do I need to do?" Herobrine asked. "Nothing much. Simply drink from this little goblet here Herobrine. Then everything will be sorted," she said pushing the goblet closer to him.

Herobrine looked in confusion at the goblet. Was he about to be poisoned? Thinking it over Herobrine questioned if it really mattered. Right now he didn't care if it was poison. In one way it might take away his pain and at the worst he would respawn very far away from here. Far away from his home far away from this pain he was feeling. Where he could make a new life for himself. Yes that's all he wanted. A new life for himself a life where this would never happen to him again.

"Come on Herobrine drink up. Don't think of yourself right now. Think about that poor girl. What they did to that poor innocent girl. She didn't deserve that did she? Standing there surrounded and shot down like that. That's not part of the game is it? And what about your dog. Did he deserve to die like that? Shot down without a thought. Monsters they are. But monsters far, far, worse than me. I would have given them a fair chance I would have let them run away. BUT NOT THEM! They come into our world, kill, plunder and feed off everything they see. They think they're so powerful. But… we'll show them what real power is Herobrine. We'll show them that they can't come here and do as they please. Won't we."

Whatever Herobrine had thought of witches in the past this one was speaking the truth. They had killed SparkleGirl. Yes, she'd been working on the greifers side. But that didn't mean she'd had to die like that. Who knew where she was respawning right now and he'd probably never see her again. Would she ever return to the world of Minecraft when she'd been treated so cruelly like that? And Wolfie his best friend, that dog had meant so much to him. He had become more of a friend than any player he'd met in Minecraft. And now they were gone. Herobrine closed his eyes and drank quickly from the flask.

Once the hot liquid hit the back of Herobrine's mouth it burned its way to his stomach and the pain was intense. All the while he was in agony he kept the image of SparkleGirl and Wolfie in his mind. Watching them being killed over and over again. This is for you! he thought to himself. Once the pain got too much Herobrine screamed out in agony and fell to the floor. Whatever the mixture was doing to him he felt like his body was being burned inside by hot lava. "AARGH MY EYES, IT'S BURNING THEM!" Herobrine screamed rubbing his eyes with the back of his hands. Then when the pain became so intense his body shut down and he fell into unconsciousness.

"Sleep Herobrine, let the rage fill every part of your body. I probably should have told you that your memory is now gone. Never will you remember your past life. All those happy memories will be long gone. But… there is one memory you'll keep for the rest of your life. Every time you see another Minecraft player you'll see that scene of your friend and dog getting killed over and over again. You'll re-live that pain and because of that you'll seek justice for it. You'll make them pay. They'll pay for what they've done to you, and also to us. Never again will they think they can come here and take what they want. You'll have your revenge Herobrine, but they'll ALL pay for it," the witch said rubbing her hands with glee.

The witch stood back when she saw Herobrine wake up. As soon as he opened his eyes she knew the old Herobrine was gone. Now instead of two pupils in his eyes, they were replaced with two eyes that burned brightly with pain, rage and destruction. "Rise my beauty. You'll have all the armies of darkness at your command now. Everyone will bow down before you. You're now a God in Minecraft. Now go seek your justice and make them all pay!" she screamed and watched as Herobrine teleported away.

"Herobrine is dead. Long live Herobrine!" the witch sneered and then disappeared to see what destruction her new creation was getting up to.

The End.

Herobrine – Birth of a Monster on Audiobook.

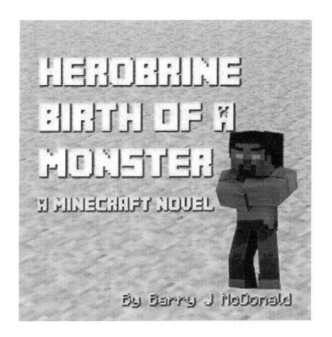

Now Available on Audible.com And iTunes.

Listen to a sample on MinecraftNovels.com

Bonus Chapter From Herobrine – Revenge Of A Monster.

SparkleGirl looked at her reflection in the river as she filled her bucket with water. It had been a year since the last time she'd seen Herobrine, but that had been the good Herobrine. The one that had taken her in when he didn't have to and the one who'd given her a home. But now that sweet, caring and helpful Herobrine was gone. She'd heard a rumour that he'd turned into a ghastly monster that now left destruction and death in his path.

"It's all my fault," SparkleGirl sobbed to herself and wiped away a tear. Why had she ever listened to ChuckBone? Why had she ever agreed to move into Herobrine's home, and then take it all from him the moment his back was turned? Look where that great plan had got her, killed and left to respawn back at square one with nothing to show for all her hard work. But although it felt hard for her to come to terms with what she'd lost. Herobrine had lost so much more. He'd lost his home, his favourite pet Wolfie and he'd lost himself. And she was to blame.

How could she ever make it up to him for what she had done? If Herobrine was as mad as people had said he was, how could she even say "sorry" to him? He'd probably cut her down with his sword the first second he saw her. Then even if she did try to apologise to him, how would she ever find him in this vast world. SparkleGirl pulled the bucket quickly from the river; she couldn't bear to look at her reflection a second longer. All it did was show her as a person who had sold herself out for a few possessions. She was nothing but a griefer.

Walking back to her home she wondered why she'd come back into the Minecraft world again. She could have walked away from this world and never returned. Did she really think she could just step back in time to those few happy days she'd had with Herobrine. Or had she come back to get revenge. She knew the first possibility would never happen. So maybe it was revenge that she was looking for. Not just for her, but also for Herobrine.

SparkleGirl had heard that ChuckBone and his gang had done well after Herobrine had disappeared. After plundering Herobrine's home and taking all they needed, ChuckBone's gang had grown from strength to strength. She'd heard that he now lived in a huge fortress that was supposed to have over a hundred Minecraft players living in it. All under ChuckBone's control. ChuckBone would love all that power, SparkleGirl thought to herself. From the short time she'd known him, she could see the big ego he had. It was never enough for ChuckBone to just live and survive in Minecraft; he wanted it ALL. He wanted power and people to do his bidding.

But maybe all that was a rumour too. There were so many rumours and lies in Minecraft, who knew what the truth was anymore. Maybe that was the same as the story about Herobrine. Could someone so good really change that much and become someone so evil. If so, where would he have got all that power from? She never remembered Herobrine having magic powers before, if he had, why he hadn't used them that day when he was almost killed by a huge spider. Only for her arrow he would've died that day. So where had he got them. The only ones that practised evil magic like that were the witches. But where had Herobrine met a witch, and why would she ever give him special powers. It just didn't make sense to her.

SparkleGirl looked up from what she was doing and saw that the cubic sun was starting to lower in the sky. Having not much else to do, she took her time going back inside her home. It was peaceful at this time of day, but it also meant that the hostile mobs weren't very far either. "Time to go boy. Let's pack it in for the day," she called over to her dog. Wolfie2 ran from where he'd been sniffing the ground to join her at her homes front gate. "Having fun?" she asked. She'd never thought of taming a wolf as a pet before, but after seeing the fun and love Herobrine had for Wolfie, she decided to try it out too. It was one of the best decisions she'd made since coming back. Wolfie2 was great company and a good watch dog. Whenever there was a hostile mob close by her she always knew about it.

Like Herobrine, she'd decided to live life in Minecraft alone now. She'd been part of a group in the past and look where that had got her. Maybe Herobrine had been right. Maybe it was best to keep to yourself and not draw attention to how well you were doing. Doing otherwise would only draw griefers towards you to take everything you'd worked hard for.

As SparkleGirl switched on the booby trap at her front door, she smiled. Herobrine had taught her well in those few days they'd been together. He'd shown her his night time routine of always checking escape tunnels and making sure weapons were in plenty. This things had saved her many times. Standing in the courtyard of her home SparkleGirl looked up at the first star in the night sky and said a quick thank you. She might never see Herobrine again, but she was glad that she'd met him. Even if it had been under false pretensions. "Come on Wolfie2, I think we've some juicy pork chops with our names on them," SparkleGirl said and headed to the furnace to cook supper. "It might be a busy night, and we'll need our energy levels high. Then it's off to bed," she said, "Who knows what's going to come to our front door tonight. But whatever it is, we'll be ready for it."

After supper SparkleGirl did a quick clean up before again, checking everything was in place, and her home was safe. She'd built her home exactly as Herobrine had designed his. So she knew that it was a tough one to get into. But even tough homes could get broken into as she had seen.

Happy that everything was now in place SparkleGirl called Wolfie2 to her. "Come on boy, bedtime!" Walking to her bedroom SparkleGirl hoped she'd sleep better than she had the night before. She'd tossed and turned with a nightmare that she couldn't shake off until Wolfie2 had woken her with his barking. She hoped tonight would be a better night.

But she was wrong.

Find Out What Happens Next In…

Available On Amazon.com and iTunes.

Thanks

Thanks for purchasing a copy of Herobrine – Birth of a Monster. If you enjoyed the book, please take a moment to leave a review. It's greatly appreciated and helps to get this book in front of more new readers.

Thank you.

Barry J McDonald

Why not drop by my Facebook page and "Like It"

https://www.facebook.com/BarrysMinecraftNovels

www.MinecraftNovels.com

Printed in Great Britain
by Amazon.co.uk, Ltd.,
Marston Gate.